WHERE DO I BELONG?

by M. Jean Craig
pictures by Ray Cruz

FOUR WINDS PRESS/NEW YORK

Published by Four Winds Press
A Division of Scholastic Magazines, Inc., New York, N.Y.
Text copyright © 1971 by M. Jean Craig.
Illustrations copyright © 1971 by Ray Cruz.
All rights reserved.
Printed in the United States of America
Library of Congress Catalogue Card Number: 75–142530

By the same author

THE DRAGON IN THE CLOCK BOX

THE LONG AND DANGEROUS JOURNEY

BOXES

NOT VERY MUCH OF A HOUSE

THE NEW BOY ON THE SIDEWALK

POMANDO

DINOSAURS AND MORE DINOSAURS

It is early morning and early morning is a good time for wondering.

"Where do I belong?" Jo-Bear wonders.

"Where do I belong?" Jo-Bear asks his mother and his father.

"You belong right here where you are," says Jo-Bear's mother.

"You belong at home with us," says Jo-Bear's father.

"You belong right here at home with us, of course," say Jo-Bear's mother and father, and they hug him. "That's where you belong."

"Yes, I do. Of course I do," says Jo-Bear.

"Now it is time for me to do my shopping," says Jo-Bear's
	mother, and she puts on her hat with the blue flowers
	and picks up her basket and out the door she goes.
"Now it is time for me to go to work," says Jo-Bear's father,
	and he puts on his leather cap and picks up his lunchbox
	and out the door he goes.
"Now it is time for me to leave for school," says Jo-Bear,
	and he puts on his red woolly hat and picks up his bag
	of sandwiches and his books and out the door he goes.
"Yes, of course I belong at home with my mother and my
	father," says Jo-Bear, and he closes the door behind him.
"But not always."

It is a bright, sunny middle-of-the-morning. A bright, sunny middle-of-the-morning is a good time for asking questions.

Jo-Bear's teacher asks questions and Jo-Bear's friends ask questions and Jo-Bear asks questions, and everyone tries to find the answers together.

At the end of the morning, Jo-Bear asks the teacher one more question.

"Where do I belong?" asks Jo-Bear. "Where do I really belong?"

"Why, you belong right here where you are," the teacher answers.

"You belong right here in school, asking questions and answering questions and learning how to grow up."

"Yes, I do. Of course I do," says Jo-Bear.

Then the bell rings and school is over and Jo-Bear puts on his red woolly hat and he runs outside with his friends.

Jo-Bear feels the warm sunshine on the ends of his ears.
Jo-Bear feels the cool breeze on the tip of his nose.
Jo-Bear feels the soft grass under his feet.
"Yes, of course I belong in school, learning how to grow
    up," says Jo-Bear.
"But not always."

It is a wild, windy afternoon.

Jo-Bear and his friends have eaten their lunch and now
they are in the playground.

Jo-Bear has taken off his red woolly hat and put it on the
ground with his books.

Jo-Bear and his friends are playing together.

They play running games and shouting games and rolling
games and sliding games.

They play teasing games and jumping games and throwing
games and hiding games.

They play fighting games and singing games and seven
other kinds of games, and then they sit down to rest.

Jo-Bear sits next to his best-of-all friend, whose name is
Clarence.

A wild, windy afternoon, after you have played and while
you are resting, is a good time to talk.

Jo-Bear and Clarence talk.

They talk about swimming next summer.

They talk about Theo's new baby sister.

They talk about a hard word on the spelling test. Clarence
spelled it wrong, but Jo-Bear spelled it right.

They talk about the ball Clarence had last year. It was a
very good ball, but now it is lost.

Then Jo-Bear asks Clarence, "Clarence, do you know
where I belong? Where I really and truly belong?"

"Well, of course I do," says Clarence. "You belong right
here where you are. You belong with Theo and with
Marcy and with Benji and Binny and with me. You
belong with your friends, of course!"

"Yes, I do. Of course I do," says Jo-Bear. "I belong right
here with my friends."

The sun is getting lower in the sky.

Theo stands up. "I have to go home now," says Theo, and he walks off.

Marcy stands up. "I have to go too," says Marcy, and she walks off.

Benji and Binny stand up together. "It's time for us to go home," say Benji and Binny together, and they walk off together.

Clarence stands up. "It's getting late. I'll see you tomorrow, Jo-Bear," says Clarence, and Clarence walks off.

Jo-Bear stands up.

He picks up his red woolly hat and his books.

He looks around at the empty playground.

"Yes, of course I belong with my friends," says Jo-Bear.

"But not always."

It is nearly the end of the afternoon.

Jo-Bear is walking home through the forest.

Jo-Bear is still wondering.

Jo-Bear is still asking himself questions.

He does not think or look which way he is going.

After a long time Jo-Bear feels tired, and stops walking.

He looks around him. He sees a big oak tree he has never
seen before.

He listens. He hears a little brook he has never heard
before.

He sniffs. His own part of the forest doesn't smell like this. He scuffles his feet on the path. His own path, through his own part of the forest, is covered with little round stones. This path is soft and sandy. His own path, the path he takes from home to school to back home again, is flat. This path slants up and up.

"*This* is not where I belong!" says Jo-Bear. "I'm lost! I didn't think and I didn't look, and now I am lost in the forest."

Jo-Bear doesn't start to run, this way or that way.

Jo-Bear doesn't sit down and cry.

Jo-Bear stands still and thinks.

"If I stay where I am, someone will find me after a while," thinks Jo-Bear. "But maybe not for a *long* while."

"If I go back, I might find my own path again," thinks Jo-Bear some more. "But I might not. I might get *very* lost, instead."

Then Jo-Bear thinks harder.

"This path slants up and up," thinks Jo-Bear. "If I follow it, I will go higher and higher. If I go high enough, I may be able to look out across the trees and see which way is home."

Jo-Bear starts to walk again, up and up the sandy path.

Suddenly the path seems darker.

Suddenly there are no more little circles of sunlight squeezing between the leaves of the trees.

Suddenly a cold wind wooshes past Jo-Bear's ears.
Suddenly Jo-Bear shivers. He stops walking and looks up.
A gray cloud has covered the sky.
"*This* is not where I belong!" says Jo-Bear. "I'm getting
    cold!" He puts on his red woolly hat and pulls it down
    over his ears and buttons his jacket. He stops shivering
    right away.
Then he starts to walk again, up and up the sandy path.
A minute later something small and wet splashes in the
    path in front of him.
Jo-Bear stops walking.
There is another tiny splash, and another, and then many
    more, on Jo-Bear's hat and his jacket and against his
    face.
"*This* is not where I belong!" says Jo-Bear. "I'm getting
    wet!"

Should he creep under a bush with big leaves? There are
no bushes with big leaves.

Should he look for a cave? There isn't time, because now
it is raining hard.

But Jo-Bear sees a big dead tree, lying flat on the ground.
Perhaps . . .

Jo-Bear runs to the big dead tree. Yes, there is a hole at
one end of it. It is not a big hole, but Jo-Bear is not a
big bear. He crawls into the hole. He stops getting wet
right away. He waits.

Soon the rain stops. Out comes Jo-Bear.

Then he starts to walk again, up and up the sandy path.

Now it is really very late in the afternoon. Jo-Bear is
    hungry,
    and hungrier,
    and very, very hungry.

At home, there would be warm honeycakes and cool milk.

Jo-Bear stops walking.

"Oh, dear! *This* is not where I belong!" says Jo-Bear. "Not
    when I'm hungry!"

Should he look for blackberries?

It is too late in the year for blackberries.

Should he look for hickory nuts?

It is too early in the year for hickory nuts.

But it is just the right time of the year for grapes.

Jo-Bear turns around slowly in the middle of the path and looks into the forest, for grapes.

He sees blackberry bushes, with no blackberries left, not any more.

He sees hickory trees, with no hickory nuts ripe, not yet.

And behind the blackberry bushes and behind the hickory trees, Jo-Bear sees grapevines.

Jo-Bear eats three, four, five bunches of ripe grapes. He stops feeling hungry right away.

Then he goes back to the path and starts to walk again, up and up and up.

It is the very end of the afternoon.

Jo-Bear has stopped walking up and up and up. Now he is
standing on the top of a rock on the very top of a high
hill.

Above Jo-Bear is the blue sky.

Over there at the edge of the sky is the setting sun, still
shining a little, red and orange and gold through the
gray clouds.

Below Jo-Bear and all around him is the green forest.

From the top of the rock on the very top of the high hill,
Jo-Bear can see all of the green forest. It is not really a
very big forest.

Down there, on the left, is the schoolhouse and the playground.

Down there, on the right, is the chimney of Jo-Bear's own house.

Jo-Bear's own house is not really very far from the rock on the very top of the high hill.

It is very easy now for Jo-Bear to see which way is home.

Jo-Bear will go home soon, but he is not going home now, not yet.

Now Jo-Bear is just standing, straight and tall and still and all alone.

Jo-Bear is standing all alone on the top of a rock on the very top of a high hill.

And Jo-Bear is thinking again.

"Sometimes I belong at home with my mother and my father," Jo-Bear thinks.

"But not always.

"And sometimes I belong in school learning how to grow up," Jo-Bear thinks.

"But not always.

"And sometimes I belong with my friends, just being friends," Jo-Bear thinks.

"But not always."

Now Jo-Bear feels like shouting, so he shouts.

"I am Jo-Bear!" he shouts.

"I am all alone!

"I am all alone on a rock on a hill!"

Jo-Bear shouts at the blue sky.

"I am Jo-Bear!

"I have a red woolly hat!

"I know how not to be cold or get wet!

"I know how not to stay hungry or lost!

"And *now* I know where I belong!"

Jo-Bear shouts at the rosy sun, shining through the clouds.

"I am Jo-Bear and I'm all alone!

"I have a red woolly hat!

"I know how to spell hard words!

"I know how to answer questions myself!

"And now I know where I *always* belong!"

Jo-Bear shouts out and far, all the way across the green forest.

"I AM JO-BEAR!

"I belong right here where I am!

"I belong with myself—I *always* belong with myself!

"That's where I really and always belong—

"I really and truly

  and *always*

    belong

      with ME!"